Detroitopia

Book One:

After Detroit

by
Cyrus Vanover

PUBLISHED BY:
Iconic Inkwell

Detroitopia
Part One: After Detroit

ISBN-13: 978-0692213681
ISBN-10: 0692213686

Printed in the United States of America

First Edition: May 2014

10 9 8 7 6 5 4 3 2 1

Be sure to visit the author's web site for updates on new book releases and other exciting things!

www.cyrusvanoverbooks.com

CHAPTER 1

W^{E DID IT}. We blew ourselves up. It was a cataclysmic event with a sting that was felt throughout the world. It rocked the very foundation of civilization and permanently altered the lives of every living being. All that lived, that is, which wasn't very many. No one was spared from the wrath of its anger. There was no mercy, nor was there any warning. It all happened in an instant, like an unexpected summer storm that appeared out of nowhere on a sunny day, drenching those who didn't see it coming and couldn't reach protective shelter in time. Except this storm was a killer.

It didn't happen the way everyone always thought it would. It wasn't a nuclear war that destroyed nearly all of mankind, although it was nuclear testing that triggered it. It wasn't a pandemic, an asteroid impact, a reversal of the earth's magnetic field, a particle accelerator mishap, or any of those other things we all used to fear. It was the eruption of a super volcano. It was the eruption of Yellowstone.

For so many years, people visited Yellowstone and were awed by its beauty, entertained by its geysers, and enjoyed the quiet tranquility of its streams, meadows, and valleys. How many ever stopped to consider that they were standing over a veritable ocean of angry magma just beneath their feet? How many realized as they watched their children laugh at the eruption of Old Faithful that the land they stood on was as thin as an eggshell when compared to the rest of the earth's crust? How many realized the very ground they stood on covered a ticking time bomb more powerful than all of the nuclear weapons ever made combined? Too few. That's how many. It was nothing more than a playground for them, a vacation spot.

Towns and villages sprung up around the majestic national park to cater to those who came to see it. The people inhabiting those places were the first to die when it happened. They were the lucky ones. Their deaths were nearly instant, like those unfortunate souls who had their lives snuffed out by the pyroclastic flow and unbreathable gasses from Mount Vesuvius centuries ago. Perhaps someday, hundreds of years from now, archaeologists will make plaster casts of their bodies, too. They will make castings of their silent screams, of mothers protecting their babies from an unknown nemesis, of those curled up in fetal positions as they struggled to inhale their last breaths. Perhaps someday.

Yellowstone didn't erupt on its own, you see. It had help, although indirectly. No one specifically set out to cause an eruption, and it wasn't the result of a terrorist attack. It was the indirect result of underground nuclear testing. The countdown to world destruction started in the Middle East, a region with a long history of instability, warfare, and strife. It all started when a certain Middle Eastern country detonated its first nuclear weapon…an underground test, of course.

For years, the leaders of this ancient nation whispered sweet nothings into the ears of other world leaders, assuring them that they were only spinning centrifuges to enrich uranium for peaceful purposes. They said it was for nuclear power, medical isotopes, and other such malarkey. Any fool could see what they were doing. Their talks of peace were nothing more than delaying tactics to give them additional time to enrich more and more uranium for a bomb.

And the world leaders bought it. Not all of them, of course, but enough decided to look the other way while the regime secretly—or perhaps not so secretly—constructed their own nuclear doomsday device. In their lust for power, the leaders of this nation wanted nothing less than to be a nuclear superpower, to thumb their noses at the world, and to control the Middle East with the fear of nuclear annihilation. "Give peace a chance," the world leaders said. "We have to give the sanctions time to work," they repeated, as the factories of doom continued enriching uranium day and night. And then it happened. They conducted a successful test of a nuclear device.

The first indication that something had happened was detected by earthquake monitoring stations around the world, although initially there was no cause for alarm or concern. According to their seismic monitoring equipment, it looked like nothing more than an earthquake, albeit a small one. It was nothing unusual to these guys, who were used to seeing small earthquakes on a daily basis all around the world.

In just a few hours, however, an announcement was made by a representative of the regime on a popular international news network, an announcement that would forever change the world. It was announced that this country had just joined the exclusive club of nuclear powers. All around the country there was great celebration. People shot guns in the air in jubilation and national pride, but there was no celebration for the fledgling nuclear power's neighbors. There was only great concern.

That one nuclear test triggered a nuclear arms race across the Middle East. To counter what was perceived as a threat to regional stability and security, a neighboring nation quickly developed and tested its own nuclear weapons, just as it had promised it would if its old rival ever had the bomb. Another neighboring nation quickly followed suit. It made no sense to its leaders to be defenseless against nuclear-armed neighbors, so it developed its own nuclear weapons program, as well.

Other nations in the region quickly followed with nuclear programs of their own. And, of course, with all of these new nuclear weapons programs, there was a large spike in underground nuclear testing. One country would test a bomb, and then a neighboring country would set out to test a more powerful bomb. And so it went, each nuclear bomb test more devastating than the previous one, each nation trying to one-up its neighbors.

What no one realized, or even considered, was the powerful pulses of energy that traveled around the world through the earth's crust every time an underground nuclear explosion occurred. Like ripples in a pond after the throw of a stone, these pulses of energy were not felt by most people, save for those closest to the blast sites. But Yellowstone noticed. With each new underground nuclear test, the ground covering the ocean of magma under Yellowstone grew weaker and weaker until it could take no more.

It wasn't an explosion so much as it was an implosion, at least at first. In an instant, thousands of acres of Yellowstone National Park fell into the boiling ocean of molten rock beneath it, instantly vaporizing those unfortunate souls who happened to be visiting the park at the time. I doubt they even had time to feel fear or to know what was happening. They had it easy; it was those who survived the ordeal who had it hard.

When Yellowstone erupted, it made a truly terrible sound that could be heard hundreds of miles away. Some say it sounded like death, a loud and terrible rumble that lasted for days. Others describe it as the sound of a terrible wailing and gnashing of teeth, straight from the pits of Hades itself. There are many who still hear it in their dreams. I suppose it will haunt them for the rest of their days. Who can ever truly be free again after such an experience? Such things change people, but never for the better.

Rivers of lava poured out of the angry caldera in all directions. Smoke, fire, and brimstone made their way toward the sky. So powerful was the calamity that the volcano created its own weather system over and around it, stretching for miles in all directions. Lightning flashed constantly across the sky, like millions of flash bulbs going off at once. Powerful winds ripped through the land. Tornadoes descended from the ominous sky above and wreaked havoc on an already-ravaged land. It truly was hell on earth.

The ash that spewed from the mouth of Yellowstone formed a dark, ominous cloud layer that covered the whole world. It poured ash and foul sulfuric rain over the lands for what felt like an eternity. I stopped counting how many days it rained before it all stopped. The rivers and streams became foul with the sulfuric muck that quickly filled them. The air became almost unbreathable from the stench of the rotting corpses mixed with sulfuric fumes. The remains of an untold number of humans and all manner of animals covered the lands. There were just too many of them to bury. I doubt anyone will ever know with certainty how many perished.

I wish I could tell you that there was plenty of food and water for those of us who survived. Oh, how I wish. But that certainly wasn't the case. At first, the survivors simply looted grocery stores, convenience stores, restaurants, warehouses... anywhere they knew they could find food. Those resources went fast, too fast. You would have thought that people would have had enough sense to conserve and ration their provisions. You would have thought.

When the easy stuff ran dry, people turned to stealing from others, or just killing them and helping themselves. Some people hunted. Just as all of humanity was not completely destroyed, many animals survived, too. But not all people had hunting skills or anything to hunt with. In time, desperation set in. Some tried to glean nutrients from eating bark, chewing on pieces of leather, eating insects, and basically anything else that would keep them alive.

When those things failed to quench their hunger, some turned to killing others and eating their flesh. There are even rumors of mothers killing and eating their own children. I have no reason to doubt that such things happened. Extreme hunger tends to make people do extreme things they never imagined they were capable of...and later deeply regret.

It has been three years now since Yellowstone erupted. News of other parts of the world travels very slowly. As far as I or anyone else knows, there are no more nations. There is no more Russia, China, Germany, Brazil, or the United States. The old boundaries no longer exist. There are no more large armies to defend them. There is, however, something new. Or something old that has been made new again. It all depends on how you look at it. We have city-states. The great cities didn't necessarily die when Yellowstone erupted.

Rather, they were transformed into small nations, many of them with their own kings and queens.

Some of these kingdoms have already waged war against neighboring kingdoms, like the recent invasion of Chattanooga by the army of Atlanta. It had something to do with the pillaging of resources. Food, medicine, alcoholic beverages, gasoline, and so many other resources are now commonly fought over. That's the usual reason behind most wars these days...something to do with acquiring resources, or preventing others from having access to the resources you control.

Even though Chattanooga had the smaller army, Atlanta wasn't able to take it, or its resources. Chattanooga's mountains gave its army a strong tactical advantage. When Atlanta's army marched up I-75 to plunder the small city, Chattanooga's army had no problem defeating it from the relative safety of their positions high up in the mountains. There have been other wars, of course, but they are of little consequence. The outcomes of those wars have no bearing on the lives of either my family or me.

My name is Adam Reese. I live in Detroit. Some call it Motor City. Others call it Motown. I call it home. Whatever you call it, it's been home to my family and me our entire lives. It's where I was born and raised, where I went to school, and where I worked. I used to work at a vehicle assembly plant for Ford Motor Company just down the road in Dearborn. Drivetrain installation was my specialty, but I could easily fill in when other areas were in a pinch. I was good at my job, and I enjoyed my work. All of that was before Yellowstone, of course.

These days, my job, if you can call it that, is hunting for fresh meat. I'm not picky, either. Rabbit, snake, squirrel, rat, groundhog...all are fair game. Hey, meat is meat when you're hungry, which is pretty much all the time. And besides, you can make nearly any animal taste great if you know how to prepare it. On a rare occasion, I bag a deer. We eat a little better for a few days, but we also give some of the meat to our neighbors and use it to trade for supplies. It's hard to watch those around you starve, and besides, the meat doesn't keep for very long anyway. May as well let others in on the bounty.

I live with my mother and my younger sister, Sarah. We take care of each other. Dad died years ago of liver disease. He loved his alcohol a little too much. Loved it to death, he did. Perhaps it's just as well that he punched out early and missed all of the Yellowstone fun.

Mom stays home most days and takes care of the home as best she can. She hasn't been in good health lately and can't do much else. Sarah collects wood from around the neighborhood for cooking and for heat. It's a bigger job than you might think. The Detroit winters are bitter cold, and anything that burns is in big demand. People have actually killed and been killed over quality firewood.

We were preppers. That's how we survived Yellowstone. But we were prepping for something very different…an economic collapse, perhaps an EMP explosion. We never imagined anything like Yellowstone would ever happen, nor did anyone else.

When the sky darkened and it started raining ash, we shut ourselves in our home and lived off the rations and water we had stored in the basement. I wish I could tell you that we didn't have to fend off anyone trying to take our food, but we did. We did what anyone would do in our situation, I think…we shot them. We had to. It was either that or let them take our food, water, and our ability to survive. I always dragged the bodies far away from the house and buried them. Thankfully, no one in my house has ever tasted human flesh. It probably doesn't hurt that my hunting skills aren't too shabby, either.

Detroit really doesn't look too much different now than it did before Yellowstone. The city had been mismanaged for decades and fallen into disrepair. Many people gave up on the city and just left, some of them abandoning their homes. It looks as run-down now as it has in years past. The look of despair on people's faces is the same, too. And then, there's the wall.

Detroit's king, King Darius, erected a large wall around the city to keep the favored in and everyone else out, including my family and me. No one is really sure who this Darius guy is or where he came from. He could have been anybody...a used car salesman, a mailman, the guy who bags your groceries. He's probably just a guy who sensed an absence of leadership after Yellowstone and inserted himself in the position. Can't blame him, I guess. I probably would've done the same if I had the opportunity.

I've never been able to make any sense out of the wall. It all seems so random and meaningless. Those who live within the wall seem to be there for no other reason than they just happened to be living there when it was built. It's the same for those living outside the wall. The only thing that makes any sense to me is that it was a way for King Darius to consolidate power. I suppose it's just easier to rule over a certain number of people who are contained within a wall than it is to rule over those who live far outside the city limits. But that doesn't mean we don't hear from them or that they leave us alone. No. Just the opposite, in fact.

They call us "outlanders" even though we don't live too far outside of the city limits. They consider anyone living outside of the wall an outlander, and we have a symbiotic relationship of sorts, if you can call it that, with those who live on the inside. The city provides outlanders who live close by with fresh water and electricity. The water in the local rivers and streams is drinkable enough these days, I suppose, but few of us dare risk it. The animals seem to survive well enough on it. The earth has a remarkable way of cleansing itself that involves nothing more than the passage of time. Take a polluted river, for instance. If you stop polluting it, the river will eventually cleanse itself. Still, it's comforting to have a source of water that you know is clean.

Electricity is generated from a series of small traveling wave reactors that were installed a few years ago. These new reactors were built to withstand a lot of punishment, so they were unaffected by Yellowstone. They are highly efficient, too. The new design allows them to operate for decades without refueling. They are beautifully engineered self-contained units. Their turbines keep spinning day after day, completely oblivious as to how the world outside their reinforced concrete casings has changed. In addition to powering lights, radios, and other necessities, much of the electricity produced by these reactors is diverted to power the large water distillation plants that clean the water and make it safe for drinking.

In exchange for electricity and fresh water, each family is responsible for providing a tribute to the king once a week in the form of a small game animal. A rabbit, groundhog, duck, or a large bird such as a crane is usually sufficient. A tribute of a deer is good for a whole month. If a family is unable to provide a tribute, regardless of the reason, the punishment is death.

Actually, the punishment for most things is death. Murder, theft, assault, pissing off the wrong person, it doesn't matter. It's a one-size-fits-all solution to all of our misdemeanors, and the Detroit sentries that patrol the streets act as judge, jury, and executioner. You don't get to have an attorney present. There are no appeals. There isn't even really a trial. The verdict is whatever the sentries decide it is. It's swift justice, if you can call it justice at all. The best thing to do is to keep your head down, mind your own business, and avoid sentries at all costs. But it's not always so easy.

It's not always possible to avoid the sentries that patrol our neighborhoods because you can't always see them. It's those damned suits they wear that make them invisible. The eggheads at MIT invented the technology, and the defense contractors perfected it. The Applied Dynamic Technologies Infantry Mark III is the latest and greatest model. I'm fairly certain it's what the sentries in Detroit are using these days. I think they got them from the old National Guard bases.

The Mark I suit was the prototype. Only a handful of those were made for testing and to market to the military. The Mark II suit was the first to go into production. It had light torso armor and good, but not great, invisibility. With the invisibility engaged, the wearer could still be seen while moving around. The faster he moved, the more visible he became.

The Mark III suit has most of the same features as its predecessor except with improved invisibility. It's still not perfect though. When engaged, a wearer achieves complete invisibility while standing still. Even the rifle he is holding becomes invisible. But when he moves around, you can see a bit of a blur, kind of like a distortion of sorts. It's as though you are looking at something and then it becomes blurry, as if you need glasses.

The Mark III suit also comes with a full face helmet. You would think that such a design would inhibit a person's vision and hearing, but in reality, it's just the opposite. Those helmets have remarkable heads-up displays that give the wearer quite a bit of information about his surroundings. The wearer powers the entire suit, too. There are no heavy batteries to carry. The suit captures the wearer's kinetic and thermal energy for what amounts to an unlimited power source. I don't even pretend to understand how any of it works. I'm just a simple car guy.

At least I used to be a car guy. Things are different now, very different. And I doubt they will ever be even remotely like they were before. My job no longer has anything to do with cars. My full-time job now is survival.

CHAPTER 2

IT IS THE BRIGHTEST DAY I can remember in ages. The sun does shine on occasion. From time to time the clouds part and we do get a few rays here and there. There would be no life at all if we were completely separated from the sun. But this day is different. There's not a cloud in the sky. Strange. The sun's rays are strong and warm. It feels so, so good to let those rays soak into my skin, like getting your first glass of cool water after spending a few days separated from it in a desert. And the grass. It's a beautiful, luscious shade of green. The birds are singing and flitting about. Butterflies are dancing amongst the wildflowers. It's a beautiful, warm spring day, and I never want it to end.

I go for a walk in this beautiful field in front of me, running my hands through the tall blades of grass as I go. There's a slight breeze, not enough to cause a chill, but just enough to blow the scent of spring my way. And oh, what a wondrous smell! It's an intoxicating mixture of wildflowers, uncut grass, moss covered rock outcroppings, and the waters of slow-moving streams lazily winding their way to unknown destinations.

And then I see her. She's off in the distance with her back to me. She's petite with very long, blonde hair, and she's wearing a long, flowing dress of a style I don't recognize. What is she doing here? She turns around and I see her face. Beautiful. I recognize her, but not really. I have a strong feeling that I know her or that I should know her, but at the same time, I don't. I don't know her name and can't recall ever seeing her before. She waves for me to come to her and I start walking in her direction.

As I approach her, I see she is smiling, as though she is happy to see me. "What are you doing here?" I ask.

"Waiting on you," she says.

"Who are you?"

She looks at me with a look of pure love, not of the romantic kind, but rather, the purest kind of love, of total acceptance, patience, and understanding. "Does it matter?" She asks.

"I don't know," I say. And I don't. I'm confused. I don't understand any of this.

"That's the problem," she says. "You don't know." I can actually feel her love now, as though it's radiating from her and penetrating me. "The more important question is: Who are you? Adam, you have spent your entire life just going through the motions, of running from your true potential. You don't know who you are or where you are going. This must change."

"I don't understand," I say.

"If you are to become a great leader, you must first abandon your fears and insecurities. Let them go. That's the first step you must take. So many are counting on you. You must not let them down."

I am alarmed and deeply concerned by this. "A great leader? Who's counting on me? Why? Who must I not let down? You must tell me!"

She slowly starts walking toward me and I can feel her love grow stronger with each step she takes. She stops in front of me and looks up to me, her head tilted slightly to one side, as if to suggest that I should somehow know. "In time, all will be revealed," she says. "For now, it is enough to know that you must find out who you are so you can understand your true potential and do what is necessary. You can't do that without first releasing your fears and letting go of your old insecurities."

"Then who am I?" I ask.

"Someone others will soon look to for guidance and to lead them," she says. She reaches a hand up to the side of my face and touches it. As she does, I feel a sense of peace radiate through me. She leans in to me, her head drawing close to mine. I close my eyes and she whispers into my ear. "They're counting on you." She kisses my cheek.

I open my eyes and take a deep breath. I immediately realize I'm lying down in my bedroom. I sense heavy breathing on the side of my face and it smells like it came straight from a sewer. I turn to see where it's coming from and am face-to-face with Juno, my dog. "Get down, Juno!" I say and give her a little nudge to get her off the bed. She jumps down and quickly turns around and stares at me with a look of innocence and anticipation. I prop myself up on an elbow to get my bearings. Was I dreaming? Was I hallucinating? What was all of that about? *A great leader? Yeah, right,* I think. *I'll be doing good to lead myself out of bed this morning.*

I am suddenly aware of a sensation of wetness on the side of my face and reach up to feel it. It's definitely wet. "Juno, did you just lick my face?" I ask. She gives a little bark as if to reply that she did. But I didn't even need to ask. I know it to be true...I've been dog-licked!

"What a lovely way to start a day," I say to myself. "Note to self...must do something about Juno's nasty dog breath."

Of course, I'm not mad at her. Can't be. I love that old pooch. She's been a great companion to me for a long time. I rescued her several years before Yellowstone from a shelter. She was just a few hours away from being sent to the great doggy afterlife in the sky when I came along. All it took was a few wags of her tail and that pitiful look on her face and she had my heart. She's a mutt, of course, not one of those pure breeds. And that's perfectly fine with me. I think mutts make the best dogs because they are so tough. It's the pure breeds that get sick all the time. But as tough as Juno is, she's starting to show her age. She's no longer a pup, that's for sure. And I can see her ribs, too. That can't be good. I try to take care of my little friend as best I can, but some days I fear it's not good enough.

I throw my covers off and sit on the side of the bed. I run my fingers through my hair and then look in my hand. It's the same as yesterday and the day before. My hand is filled with strands of hair. It's slowly but surely falling out. Stress and malnutrition will do that to a person.

I get up, walk over to the sink, and turn on the faucet. Water comes out…this time. I never know from day-to-day whether we will have water or not since it's completely out of my control. Sometimes it works…sometimes it doesn't. I wash my face to get the dog slobber off and then look in the mirror at my unshaven face. I look old, much older than I actually am anyway. Stress and malnutrition will do that to a person, too.

I start to get dressed and put on a pair of jeans. I catch a glimpse of myself in a full-length mirror and I realize for the first time that I now have a great set of abs. I laugh. It strikes me as funny, because I've always wanted a great set of abs. What guy doesn't? But not like this. I used to dream of going to the beach, stripping off my shirt, and having to fend off the women because of my chiseled physique. Well, it looks like I finally have the abs I've always wanted, but the rest of me doesn't look so great, kind of emaciated actually. *I'm in no danger of being attacked by a horde of beautiful women looking like this*, I think. Like I ever was before. It's that whole stress and malnutrition thing again.

I look out my bedroom window and see Detroit in the distance. Well, I can see some of it. The wall surrounding the city blocks much of my view. No matter, it's not much to look at anyway. The sky is dark an ominous as it usually is. Another beautiful day in the neighborhood. I quickly finish getting myself together.

I step out of my bedroom and enter the living room. That's what I call it, anyway. Our house is very small. It only has two bedrooms. I sleep in one, while Mom and Sarah share the other. Our kitchen and living room are more or less one room with nothing separating them. And, of course, the basement was perfect for storing the food, water, and supplies that allowed us to survive Yellowstone. Even though we couldn't afford much when we bought this house, I'm still very thankful for it. It has served us well.

Sarah and Mom are already up. Sarah is tending to a fire in our wood burning stove. "It's about time you drug your lazy bones out of bed," she says. "Are you going to do anything productive today or just lounge around? Would you like me to bring you a cocktail to start the day off right?"

She's teasing, of course. She's a great sister and I love her dearly. But I also worry about her. I worry about what kind of future she has, if any. Will she be able to marry and have a family of her own? Even if it's possible, does it even make sense for her to start a family of her own the way things are now? I don't know. She's only 16. She didn't even get to start high school, let alone finish. There are no more organized schools. She's highly intelligent, though. The girl has street smarts and that's what really counts these days.

"Too early for a cocktail, twisted sister," I say. "But lounging around all day does sound appealing. Where do I sign up?"

Sarah smiles. It's funny because we both know that taking a day off is never an option. There's work to do…always is. She'll spend her day gathering wood for the fire and taking care of other chores around the house. I'll spend my day hunting for food and a tribute. Mom will stay here and protect everything from looters. There's enough work to keep all of us very busy.

Mom is cooking something in a pot on the stove. She's thin like the rest of us, but she's also aged a lot in the past few years. She's only 47, but, honestly, some days she looks much older. I worry about her, too. I grab my boots and start to put them on.

"You can't leave without eating something first," Mom says. "I'm boiling some eggs for us right now." She's still a typical mom, always nagging me to eat something before I leave.

"Sounds good," I say and sit down at the table to await my feast of one single hard boiled egg. Mom does some sewing and other things for a family that has a few chickens. It's been a lifesaver for us more than once.

I take my time eating breakfast, chewing slowly and savoring each bite. I've found that if I eat very slowly, it tricks my mind into thinking it's a bigger meal than it really is. I get a greater sense of fullness in my belly like that. I trick myself in other ways, too. Like when we don't have enough wood to build a fire large enough to heat the house.

When it's time to go to bed and I'm lying under the covers shivering, I just imagine myself taking a walk on a nice, warm beach in the summer. It works. I concentrate on feeling the sun's warm rays on my skin and eventually forget about being cold. Some nights, it's the only way I can go to sleep. I've gotten really good at practicing mind over matter. It helps me tolerate things better. Perhaps I'm really a psychologist in another life.

Breakfast is over much too soon, as it usually is. I slam down two glasses of water to help fill my belly a little more and then grab my crossbow. I only hunt with a crossbow because I can easily retrieve and reuse the bolts. I'm a good shot with it, too. We have a shotgun, but I always leave it with Mom so she can use it to protect our home if necessary, which lately seems to be happening more frequently. And besides, people seem to be more intimidated by the shotgun than they are by the crossbow. I've never understood the logic behind that since both can kill you.

There's also the ammunition issue. If I hunt with the shotgun, I'll quickly use up all of our ammunition. And then what will I do? Go to the store and buy some more? Not likely. There's no big box store I can go to for supplies. People trade what few things they have with others, but that's about it. Ammunition is very hard to come by.

"Bring home a deer, Adam," Sarah says as I walk out the door.

"Will do, Sis." She sends a reassuring smile my way. "Today is deer day," I say and then turn and walk out. It's time to go to work.

CHAPTER 3

I START WALKING ON MY usual route to the fields. At least that's what I call them. Even though we're technically outside the city wall, we're still very much in an urban area. A field to me is any open area where I might find a rabbit, groundhog, or some other furry critter looking for a morsel to eat. Before Yellowstone, many open areas were created when abandoned homes were torn down. That's where I'm heading now. I know of a good place just off Market Street not far from the old Fisher Town Center.

As I walk to my destination, I pass by an old man sitting on the side of the road. At least I think he's old. It's been ages since he's shaved. It makes it hard to determine his age. He reaches both arms out to me as if he's trying to grab something invisible in the air. "Help me, please," he says. "Please give me something to eat. I'll take anything you've got. Help me, please."

He looks thinner than I am, if that's even possible. Filthy, too. Probably hasn't had a shower in months. I keep walking. My heart breaks for him, but there's not a thing in the world I can do. He's just one of many who cry out for help. From the way he looks, he won't last too much longer, and when he goes I suspect he'll become a meal for others like him. I try not to think about it. I try imagining that I'm walking alone on a path in a beautiful forest. The Appalachian Trail. Yes, that's it! Mind over matter.

I turn a corner around an abandoned building and immediately see the corpse of a man hanging on a wooden cross. He's been there a few days. This isn't the first time I've seen him. Still, you never really get used to seeing such things...or smelling them.

The buzzards have been snacking on him and it's a gruesome site. He's already missing his eyeballs, his nose, and little bits and pieces of flesh here and there. What's left of his face is a mess of dried blood and torn flesh. I don't even remember what he did to earn such a punishment. Not that it matters. Even the slightest infraction means death these days. It's best to just keep your head low, turn in your weekly tribute, and keep to yourself. I'm just hoping someone will have mercy on the poor guy and torch his body in the middle of the night like they did the last guy. Burning the body would also get rid of that nasty stench, and that would be doing the whole neighborhood a favor.

Punishment didn't always mean death on a cross. That's a fairly recent development. The sentries used to be efficient in the administration of their punishments. They would simply take the guilty, tie him or her to a post, and quickly dispatch that person with a bullet to the head. I'm not saying that such a thing is right, only that a bullet to the brain means that the recipient doesn't feel any pain and that death is instant. Well, that's how it usually works. It's not like it is in the movies. A bullet to the brain doesn't always mean instant death. Sometimes a second bullet is necessary to do the job. Still, it's a preferable alternative to what we have now.

This whole crucifixion thing is something new and nasty. I think the sentries are bored and like the idea of watching people die slow, agonizing deaths. It's entertainment to them. I suspect others fancy themselves as some sort of modern-day Roman soldiers, and no Roman soldier is complete without getting a crucifixion under his belt.

I quickly walk past the dead man to get away from the stench of rotting flesh. The field I plan on hunting in is not far. Almost there. When I arrive, I'll find a nice spot, settle in, and wait for something to come along foraging for food.

Out of the corner of my eye I see the brick on the side of a nearby building blur, almost as if the brick moved or something. A sentry? I can feel my heart beating faster. Without thinking, I turn my head and look, not that it'll do any good. You can't see them when they are standing still. I don't see anything. I quickly turn my head back around, look straight ahead, and continue walking. *Keep your head down and keep to yourself*, I tell myself. Don't want to attract any unwanted attention.

"Citizen of Detroit! Halt!" I hear from behind me. I stop dead in my tracks. I'm sure it was intended for me. I can feel my heart beating even faster. My body feels as though a massive adrenaline surge just shot through it. The fight or flight response is kicking in and I have to suppress it. If I try to either fight or flee, I'm a dead man. It's been awhile since my last encounter with a sentry. I suppose I'm past due for another. I slowly turn around and before me is a fully visible Detroit sentry with an M4 carbine rifle slung over one shoulder. In his right hand is a police baton.

"Where do you think you're going with that?" he asks as he taps my crossbow with his baton.

"To hunt for a tribute for his majesty," I say while looking down at the ground in front of me. I try to look as reverent and respectful as possible. "And for food for my family." It's a perfectly reasonable excuse and it's the truth. The crossbow isn't even loaded. The bolts are safely stored in the quiver mounted underneath it.

"How do I know you're not looking for trouble?" he asks. "You could sure cause a lot of trouble with a piece like that."

I keep my eyes lowered. I can feel my palms becoming sweaty. "I'm not a troublemaker, sir. I'm just a poor servant of the king looking for a tribute."

"And a little something for yourself," he adds.

"Yessir."

The sentry extends his baton and places it underneath my chin. He lifts my head until I'm staring into the empty void of his helmet visor. "You stink," he says. "You need a bath."

I say nothing in return.

"Where will you be hunting?" he asks.

"In that field by the old water tower." I turn and look at it. "It's not far."

"Very well, then. Go and do your hunting. Let's see what you bring back for the king." He lowers his baton and I turn and start walking toward the field again.

That wasn't so bad, I think. *It could have been much worse, like that time when...*

I hear a loud, cracking sound, almost like the sound of a baseball hit by a bat. At the same time, I feel a sharp, stinging sensation surge through my body from the back of my right thigh. In an instant, I completely lose my ability to stand and fall to the ground. I writhe in unbelievable pain for a few seconds before I realize what just happened. The sentry has hit me in the back of my leg with his baton.

I lie on the ground for what feels like an eternity as the searing pain subsides. I slowly pick myself up and stand again. Of course, the sentry is nowhere to be seen. I'm sure he's nearby watching and laughing to himself. I'm nothing more than entertainment to him, just a little something to break the monotony of an otherwise boring day of patrol. I pick my crossbow up and continue walking, hobbling actually, toward the field.

I make it to the field and take cover in my usual spot, a great little place I found one day. It gives me a great field of view but provides a lot of cover at the same time. I lean my back against the brick wall of a building and look through the bushes at the empty field of uncut grass in front of me. Nothing yet. I pull a crossbow bolt out of its quiver, load it, and wait.

My leg is still throbbing. I run my hand over the back of my thigh. It stings. *That's going to leave a nasty mark*, I think. The sentries are getting worse. They used to stick closely to enforcing the law. The law, of course, being whatever King Darius says it is. In time they became emboldened, or bored, or both, and started harassing people. And now we have the crucifixions to deal with. They are out of control, and I am starting to worry about what's in store for us next. I don't want to be involved with any of it. I just want to live a simple life, like my family and I always have.

I see movement in a clump of grass on the far side of the field. I slowly raise the crossbow to a shooting position and look through the scope. Nothing yet. And then I see it again, movement. Yes, there's definitely something there. The only question is what. And then I see it, or them, I should say. Three rabbits come out of the clump of grass into an open area. Oh, and they're nice and plump, too.

I take my time and aim for the largest of the three. No use getting in any hurry and missing the target. I place the crosshair across my prey's center mass, slowly exhale, and gently squeeze the trigger. In an instant, the bolt flies from my crossbow and lands squarely in the rabbit's upper torso. Its death is instant. The other two rabbits scurry away from the downed rabbit and move closer to me. *This is my lucky day*, I think as I slowly ready another bolt.

Like before, I place the crosshair across the center mass of the larger rabbit, slowly exhale, and gently squeeze the trigger. Another hit! But wait… it doesn't appear to be a kill. The rabbit is still moving. It's lying on its back and I can see its legs moving, like it's trying to run away, but its legs aren't touching the ground. I quickly run over to it and see the bolt has hit it in the belly. I take my hunting knife and quickly finish the job as humanely as I possibly can. I hunt for food, not for sport, and I never want to see any living thing suffer. This includes the animals I hunt, my dear sweet dog, Juno, and all of the people who are now being tormented by the sentries. Sometimes I feel like I've seen enough suffering to last several lifetimes.

I retrieve the bolts I just shot, clean them, and return them to their home in the quiver. I gather the two rabbits I just killed, gut them with my hunting knife, and start walking home with my prize: a solid meal for my family and a tribute for the king. Aside from the abuse I took from the sentry and his baton, it's been a good day of hunting.

CHAPTER 4

I WALK SAFELY PAST THE area where the sentry harassed me earlier. Either he's no longer there, or I'm no longer interesting to him. It doesn't matter. I just want to get home with my fresh kills. Mom will take one of them and start preparing it for dinner this evening. I can already taste it…fresh rabbit cooked with some wild greens. Sarah will gather some fiddleheads and ramps, maybe a little chicory to go with our meal. Delicious! My mouth is already watering. While they are preparing one rabbit, I'll take the other and turn it in as my family's weekly tribute. I'm thankful these are nice and plump. The sentries tend to give me a hard time when I turn in animals that are lean, not that I have any choice in the matter. I do the best I can.

But before I go home, there's one order of business that I simply must take care of. I take an alley between two buildings and walk nearly two miles out of my way on a side road. I could have taken a more direct route home, but to me it's totally worth it. I will walk by Dr. Bradshaw's house and see if I can catch a glimpse of his daughter, Elise.

I've known Elise for years. Well, if I'm being honest, I should say that I know *of* her. I first met Dr. Bradshaw as one of his patients when I fell from a ladder and broke my arm trying to catch myself as I hit the ground. I think he's an excellent doctor, and I've only heard good things from others about him, as well. Elise was there that day in his office. While he was placing a cast on my arm in one of his examination rooms, she was sitting in the office reading a book. I could see her through the open door, and I couldn't stop staring. Her petite figure with long, strawberry blonde hair, her beautiful full lips and her eyes, oh her eyes! They are some of the biggest, greenest eyes I've ever seen. Gorgeous!

I don't think she saw me staring at her so much as she sensed it. As I was watching her read, she slowly looked up and her eyes met mine. It was too late for me to look away. She gave me a big, beautiful smile and then went back to reading her book. It's a good thing the doctor didn't check my pulse right then. I would've had a lot of explaining to do. I decided at that moment that she was the most beautiful girl I'd ever seen, and I still believe that very much all these years later. You see, I...

I love her.

I think about her often. Sometimes when things get really bad, I imagine being with her, talking to her, holding her in my arms and it keeps me going. I see her in my dreams, too. Does she ever think about me? I doubt it. I've never had an actual conversation with her. The best I can manage to do when I walk by her house and I see her is to smile, wave, and keep walking, like I'm just passing by. I know I should stop and talk to her one day, but what would I possibly say to her?

It's not like I can just ask her out on a date. Where would we go? What would we do? There are no restaurants, or movie theaters, or much of anything else for that matter. I'm not even sure how two people become a couple these days. All the rules have changed and I no longer know what they are. And even if I were able to have something with her, what could possibly come from it? What could I possibly give her other than my love? I feel like I have nothing I could possibly offer her other than the life of meager existence I currently have, and that's not much of a life at all.

As I approach Dr. Bradshaw's house, I quickly realize that I'm in luck. Elise is outside hanging clothes on a line to dry. She has always been petite, but she's looking sickly thin these days. Her clothes are hanging off her as though her body is a coat hanger. And her hair...it looks matted in places and tangled in others. Her face, arms, and hands look dirty. I'm sure she gets to take a shower or bath about as often as anyone else does, which isn't often enough. Her eyes look weak, as though part of who she is—or was—has been stolen from her. Still…I can't help but think she's so beautiful.

I walk at a slow but deliberate pace past her with my crossbow in one hand and the two rabbits in the other. I try to look casual as I look over in her direction. Yes…YES! She has noticed me and is looking in my direction. She smiles that incredible smile and I smile back.

"Hi," I say. I almost can't believe it. It's the first thing I've ever said to her. One single word. My heart is beating fast now. I see her mouth moving in reply but can't hear what she's saying. Her voice is too soft, too faint. I assume she has said "hi" back and keep walking. Some Romeo I am. I can't even bring myself to strike up a conversation with this incredible girl. Still, that smile she gave me made it all worth it. I'll be seeing that smile when I drift off to sleep tonight. Baby steps, I tell myself, baby steps.

I get some distance from her on the road and look back. She's looking in my direction, and then I see the expression on her face change to one of horror, as though she's just seen something truly awful. She quickly runs into her house. I turn around to see what has startled her and a sentry is standing right in front of me. If I had taken just two more steps, I would have walked right into him.

"Where are you going with those, outlander?"

"Fresh kills, sir. One is a tribute to his majesty, the king. The other will be a meal for my family." As before, I look to the ground when speaking as a sign of deference. My disdain for the sentries is growing as each day passes, but I don't want any trouble, either.

"I'll take those for you, both of them," he says. "I'll make sure you get credit for this week and the next."

"I mean no disrespect, sir, but if possible I would prefer to drop my tribute off at the usual place."

This is highly unusual. I have never heard of a sentry accepting a tribute while on patrol. I'm not sure what he's up to.

"Then it's not possible," he says. He raises his police baton and extends the end of it into my chest. "If you don't want any trouble, then turn them over."

I don't say anything in reply. I don't even know what to say.

"What's the matter, don't you trust me?" His tone is mocking.

Just behind him, I notice a distortion in my field of vision and then another sentry appears, but this one is different. His sentry suit is the same, but he's the tallest person I've ever seen. *He must be nearly seven feet tall*, I think. My first reaction is not one of fear, but rather of curiosity. *Where did they get a suit to fit this guy?*

The tall sentry starts walking toward me. The other sentry steps aside, leaving no question as to who is in charge. He walks right up to me and looks down at me through his helmet visor. I tilt my head back and look up to him. It feels as though I'm looking up at the sky. He doesn't say anything. Instead, he slowly raises his hands to his helmet and disconnects the data and power cable connecting it to the suit. He then takes both hands and slowly lifts his helmet off his head. He has a dark complexion, a full beard, and a shaved head. He looks down at me, his eyes looking straight into my eyes. His appearance is intimidating.

"Drop your weapon," he says.

I drop it. Not that it matters. It isn't even loaded.

"I understand you are having a bit of a trust issue, is that right?"

"N-n-no," I manage to say. "That's not it at all. It's just that…"

The sentry grabs my shirt with both hands and lifts me up until I am face-to-face with him. His strength is tremendous. He's not even straining. He never takes his eyes off mine. "That's the problem with you outlanders. You don't trust us. Do we not take care of you? Do we not provide you with clean water and electricity? And all we ask in return is a little tribute, a little respect, and a little trust. That's not so hard now, is it?"

"No," I say. But I'm not sure it's as simple as he says.

"Then drop those rabbits."

I drop them.

"We'll take care of them for you; make sure you get credit for them."

He smiles a large, mostly toothless smile. It's a smile that says "I win, you lose." He lifts me higher, turns and walks toward the side of a brick building, and throws me into it. I hit the brick hard and pain instantly shoots through my back and the back of my head. I fall to the ground and struggle to breathe.

I try to hold my head up and look around, but the pain in my head is more than I can bear. My vision is blurry, too. This can't be good. I don't hear the sentries leave the area, but they must be gone. I don't hear any activity around me. I am certain of one thing: They have taken my tribute and my family's dinner and I am not happy. And I certainly don't trust them, either. I feel so very sleepy and am having trouble holding my eyes open. I close them and let the darkness take over.

CHAPTER 5

I OPEN MY EYES AND realize I am still alive, but I'm also still in severe pain, mostly in the back of my head. I'm breathing much better now, though. I don't know how long I was unconscious. It could have been five minutes, thirty minutes, or two hours. It doesn't matter. I see a crowd of people in the distance staring at me. *Why don't they come over and help me?* I wonder. Probably too afraid of being seen by the sentries offering assistance. They would be risking death if they offered help. Can't blame them, I guess.

I prop myself up on an elbow to get my bearings and then scoot over to the brick wall, bringing myself to a sitting position against it. I feel the back of my head and don't feel any blood, but there's one heck of a lump on it. I laugh to myself. The irony of the situation doesn't escape me. I've now been beaten by sentries on two separate occasions today...and I'm not even trying to be provocative. I just want to be left alone to live a simple life. I'm not sure how much more of this "peace" I can take.

I see a man make his way through the crowd and walk over to me. *Is he mad*, I wonder? *Does he not realize he's risking his life?* I try to yell at the man to stay back but my raised voice sounds like unintelligible garble. As he comes closer, I realize who it is. I know him!

"Are you causing trouble again, Adam?" Dr. Bradshaw asks with a sly smile.

"I'm not sure if I'm causing it, but I do seem to be attracting it," I say. "I took a good hit in the back of my head."

Dr. Bradshaw examines the back of my head with his hand. "Indeed you did," he says. "You're going to need to put some ice on that for awhile."

"I don't have any ice. No one does."

"Oh, I might know of someone who has a little ice."

"Who?"

"Why, me, of course."

I stare at him, incredulous. No one I know of has access to enough electricity to keep an ice machine running.

"Come on, let's get you up," he says. Dr. Bradshaw puts one of his arms underneath mine and helps me stand. "And now let's get you to my place so we can take care of you." We start walking to Dr. Bradshaw's home, but I have to hold on to him for support. The world around me is moving in ways it shouldn't. I feel disoriented. The crowd disburses as we near his home.

I walk through the front door of Dr. Bradshaw's home and immediately realize it doesn't look like a home at all. It looks like a hospital. I see three people lying down on hospital beds in the middle of the living room. They look very ill and have all manner of medical equipment hooked to them…IV lines, oxygen cannulas, urine catheters, and other things I don't even recognize or understand. There is medical equipment everywhere. Elise is tending to one of the patients. She turns and smiles a quick smile in my direction and then quickly turns her attention back to her patient.

Dr. Bradshaw directs me to an empty bed. "You can lie down here and I'll get an ice pack for you."

I lie down as Dr. Bradshaw leaves the room. I watch Elise take care of her patient while I'm waiting. She adjusts the flow rate on an IV line and then checks some kind of patient monitoring device. There is no hesitation in her actions. She works as though she's been doing this for a long time. I've never heard of her having any formal training as a nurse or any other type of medical profession. She must have learned all of this on the job helping her father care for all the sick and injured after Yellowstone. I can't help but be impressed.

Dr. Bradshaw returns with an ice pack. "Hold this on that lump on the back of your head," he says. I place the ice pack over the lump and feel immediate relief. "Now, are you hurting anywhere else?"

"The back of my right thigh," I tell him. "A sentry hit me there earlier with his baton."

"You *have* been causing trouble, Adam. We'll have to take a look at it then. Take your pants off. Go ahead and take your shirt off, too." I look at Dr. Bradshaw and then look over at Elise. "Go ahead, take them off. This is a medical facility," he says.

I take my shirt and pants off and lie on the bed while Dr. Bradshaw examines the back of my leg. Out of the corner of my eye, I see Elise turn around and look my way and then quickly turn back to her patient. *I'm glad I wore underwear today,* I think. *This is embarrassing enough as it is.*

"The wound is superficial," he says. "It'll hurt for a few days, but I don't think any serious damage was done. Keep holding the ice on your head and I'll get something for your pain."

"Dr. Bradshaw?" I ask.

"Yes, Adam."

"Where did all of this equipment come from? And the electricity? My family barely gets enough to run a few light bulbs and a radio, and—"

"You're wondering why they give me more electricity than others, right?" I nod in the affirmative. "Well, it's not because they care about any of us, that's for sure. They do it because it benefits them, you see. I was given permission to take equipment from the old veteran's hospital to care for people here in my home. My electricity usage isn't monitored. They want us to be healthy, Adam. If we're sick, we can't provide them with fresh meat, can we?"

"No, I suppose not."

"Now, let me get those pain meds for you."

Dr. Bradshaw leaves the room again. Elise is still tending to her patient, an elderly man. I can't tell if he's unconscious or just sleeping. Regardless, he doesn't look well at all. I don't even notice Dr. Bradshaw walk back into the room or notice how long he's been gone. I even manage to completely forget about the pain in my head and thigh as I watch Elise work. Without a doubt, she is highly skilled in the art of medicine, but there's something more to it than that.

It's clear to me that everything she does is done with a great deal of compassion. She really cares about this man, whoever he is. For years, I've admired this girl from afar for her beauty, but I now realize there's so much more to her than that. I want very much to get to know her. I sense that she's every bit as beautiful on the inside as she is on the outside. I'm not sure if I'll ever get that opportunity, though.

"Here, take these," Dr. Bradshaw says as he extends his hand to me. Inside his open palm are two pills. I have no idea what they are. "Give it about twenty minutes and you'll completely forget about any pain." I take the pills out of his hand and toss them in my mouth. He hands me a glass of what I assume is water to wash it down. I take the glass and take a large drink from it. The taste shocks me, and in my surprise I almost spit it out. It's clearly not water, but it's a taste I'm all too familiar with, although it's been several years since I've had it.

"It's milk," I say. "Where in the world did you, I mean, how on earth did—"

"Adam, do you remember how the sentries don't monitor our electricity because we take care of the sick here? Well, let's just say that we have access to a few extras that others in our community are unable to acquire. Milk is good for sick people. It's good for you. Now, drink up."

I put the glass back to my mouth and slowly drink the cold, delicious liquid, savoring each drop. It's the best thing I've ever tasted in my life,

I'm sure of it. I set the empty glass down on a table beside me.

"I should probably go now," I say. "I don't want to overstay my welcome. And since I now have nothing to take home as a meal for my family, thanks to the sentries, I'll have to return to the fields and see if I can kill something else before the day is over. Otherwise, it'll be a hard day for them. Dr. Bradshaw, how can I ever repay you for —"

"You don't owe me a thing," he says. "But I do want to talk to you about something before you leave." Dr. Bradshaw takes a nearby chair and places it directly in front of me. He sits down and looks straight into my eyes. "Adam, do you want to keep living like this?"

"Like what?" I say. I don't fully understand what he means.

"Do you want to live a life where you have to live in constant fear of the sentries, of being abused, harassed, and beaten for no reason? Do you want to continue paying tribute to an unseen, unknown king?"

"No, of course not," I say. "But what can I do about it? I'm just one man."

"There are many others who are tired of it, too. Individually there's nothing that can be done, but if we fight together then —"

"Everyone's tired of the sentries, but how could we ever fight them when they have those suits? They can disappear at will."

"Perhaps we can do more about it than you might think," he says. Dr. Bradshaw's brow is furled, his eyes are serious. "Here's how you can repay me. I want you to come to a meeting this evening at the Motor City Community Center at 7 p.m. Use the back entrance."

"That's just off of Ashley Lane, right?"

"That's right."

"What's this meeting about?"

"You'll see, Adam. I'll reveal everything at the meeting. Look, I really want you to be there. There's something very special I want you to see. Promise me you'll come."

I hesitate. I feel like Dr. Bradshaw is up to something, but I don't know what. I'm not sure if I want to be involved in anything that might endanger either my family or me. Still, I feel like I owe him some sort of payment for taking care of me, and of course there's a chance that Elise might be there, too, although I don't dare ask. "Okay, I'll be there," I say, but my voice wavers.

Dr. Bradshaw's face relaxes as though my answer satisfies him. "Very good, Adam. You won't be disappointed. And, of course, I'm sure you understand the importance of discretion about this meeting."

"Of course."

I stand up, turn to leave, and feel a hand on my arm. I turn around and see Elise looking into my eyes. "I'll see you this evening, Adam."

Elise will be there! I think. There's no way I'd miss it now. I try to act like I'm not excited. "See you there," I say and nod my head. I leave Dr. Bradshaw's home.

CHAPTER 6

I HOBBLE OUT OF DR. Bradshaw's home and look behind me to see if I can see Elise one more time. I do. I can barely see her through the door as Dr. Bradshaw closes it. I'll hold onto that image in my mind until I see her again at the meeting tonight.

What on earth does Dr. Bradshaw have in mind, I wonder. Whatever it is it doesn't sound like something I want to get involved in. Going up against the sentries in those super-suits they wear sounds like suicide to me.

I'm not sure what kind of pills Dr. Bradshaw gave me, but my pain has completely vanished. In fact, I'm starting to feel very good, almost euphoric. I start walking back to the field to see if I can kill something else so my family and I can have a good meal today. A breakfast of one single boiled egg doesn't exactly hold one over for very long. We've gone days without meals before. It's no fun, and it never gets any easier. As thin as we all are right now, I'm not sure how many more meals we can afford to miss. So, back to the field I go. I'll take anything at this point. It sure beats starving any day.

Anything. I stop walking and think for a moment. No, I don't need to kill just anything, I decide. What I really need is something the sentries won't have any interest in. A rat...yes, that's it! If I kill a rat they'll give it a complete pass. And besides, rats really aren't all that bad. Kind of tastes like squirrel or maybe chicken if you use your imagination a little. And I know just the place to find them, too...the old Ryker Landfill. There's still plenty of exposed garbage there, a veritable feast if you're a rat. It's not that far, either. I start walking toward the landfill.

Like most things in the greater Detroit area, the Ryker Landfill looks as though it's stuck in time. Mounds of trash are standing by, ready to be buried by bulldozers that may or may not ever run again. Several dump trucks filled with trash wait in line to empty their loads. I suspect they'll have a very long wait. I walk over to the landfill office, which really isn't much more than a shack. Several of the windows are broken, no doubt by looters looking for anything they can use, barter, or eat.

The office door isn't fully closed. I give it a little push and it slowly opens, making a loud creaking sound as it does. I slowly walk in. A layer of thick dust covers everything, which isn't much.

It's a small office with a simple filing cabinet, a desk, a mini fridge, and a coffee maker, its pot filled with what looks to be a thick layer of mold. I open the mini fridge and look in. There's a brown paper bag in it. Someone's lunch, most likely. I take the bag out and open it. Sometimes a person can get lucky and find something that is still edible, if it was packaged the right way.

I look in the paper bag and see a sandwich bag. I pull it out to get a better look at it and just as soon as it hits what little light is in the room, I see that it's also completely covered with a thick layer of mold, whatever it is…or was. Looks like there's nothing here of any value. If there was, the looters probably already got it. I throw the bag back in the fridge and close the door.

I walk over and look out through a broken window. A slight breeze is blowing from the direction of the landfill. The smell is strong, almost more than I can handle. It smells like a rotting corpse. I've certainly smelled plenty of them to know, but it's probably just rotting garbage. At least that's what I tell myself. It's a calming and reassuring thought. Mind over matter.

I decide this is a good place to hunt. I can stay inside this building to conceal my movements and shoot through the broken window. Perfect. I load a bolt into my crossbow, place it on the window sill pointing out into the mound of garbage before me, and wait. In the far distance, down the road I traveled to get here, I see a crowd of people gathering, although I can't see what it is they find so interesting.

Like earlier, I don't have to wait long. After just a few minutes, a rat scurries out and starts nibbling on some garbage. It's a big one, too. It's easily the size of a house cat. The rats here are well fed. It'll make for a very nice meal. I carefully take aim, release a bolt, and watch it fly through the air. My eyes widen in anticipation as it nears its target and then...misses. The rat quickly scurries away behind an old tire. I quickly load another bolt and wait.

Only a few short minutes pass before I see a small head appear from behind the tire. It carefully examines its surroundings, then slowly returns to whatever it was nibbling on, and continues its meal. *Either it's very, very hungry or whatever it's eating is very, very good,* I think as I raise my crossbow, take aim, and release another bolt. It flies through the air and penetrates my prey's head. In an instant, all movement ceases. A perfect kill.

I quickly retrieve my bolts, gut the rat, and start walking home. I want to make sure I get this fresh kill home before I have to leave for Dr. Bradshaw's meeting. I'm very curious to see what he has in mind, although I'm still not sure if I want to get involved. Things are dangerous enough as it is. Getting involved in any sort of rebellion would put my family in danger, and that's something I simply can't do. I start walking home.

The crowd of people I noticed just a few moments ago has grown larger. They have most likely gathered to watch an animal fight of some kind, probably chickens or dogs. People are starved for entertainment these days and gambling over animal fights has become very common. I hate all of that stuff and try to stay away from it. I could take another route home to avoid it but it would add too much time to my trip, and I don't have much time to spare. I decide to walk through the crowd. There are enough people gathered now, so I should be able to slip through without drawing any attention to myself.

As I continue toward the crowd, I see what all of the commotion is about and my heart sinks. An execution is taking place. There's no way I can slip through the crowd and continue on my way now. These executions are public for a reason…to instill fear into the hearts and minds of the outlanders. If anyone is in the vicinity of an execution, watching is mandatory. Few people bother trying to hide from them anymore. The risk is too great. To be seen walking away from an execution would be inviting trouble, and that's certainly not what I want. So, watch this grisly affair I will. I have no choice. I move to an area near the back of the crowd to avoid attracting any unwanted attention.

There are two sentries guarding a man with a long unkempt beard and hair. His clothes are in tatters. His hands and feet are bound. He is breathing heavily, and he is visibly shaking. I don't know what crime he has committed, nor do I care. It doesn't even matter. I'm sure it was not something that deserves the punishment he is about to receive.

Two men are assembling a wooden cross on the ground, probably volunteers from the crowd. They are furiously hammering two large wooden beams together. Sometimes, the sentries will pick a couple of men from the crowd and force them to do this terrible work, but it's rare that there aren't any takers. Those who do this work are exempt from turning in tributes for an entire month. It's an offer that's hard for most to refuse.

The wood they are using is rough-cut, probably lumber stripped from some old warehouse. A thick layer of rust covers the nails they are using. The loud sound of hammering stops and one of the men looks to the sentries and indicates with a nod of the head that they are ready.

"Proceed," one of the sentries says.

The two men stand and walk to the condemned man. They each grab one of his arms and start directing him toward the cross on the ground. The man hobbles a couple of steps and then stops. His body is shaking almost uncontrollably now.

"No!" the man yells. "Have mercy on me! I beg you!"

"C'mon," one of the men holding him says. "Don't make this hard on yourself or on us." The two men pull on his arms for him to continue but he doesn't move.

"I have a wife and children," he says. "Who will take care of them? How will they eat?" The man starts wailing, his voice now an uncontrolled howl of despair emanating from the very depths of his soul. The two men pull harder on his arms and he falls to his knees.

"C'mon, now. Let's just get this over with," one of the men says.

The condemned man stays on his knees and continues wailing. The two men drag him over to the wooden cross lying on the ground and position him on it. The man stops wailing, swallows hard, and then goes silent. He appears to have accepted his fate. Any remaining fight left in him is now gone and he just stares blankly into the sky above him. The two men take leather straps and tie his body to the wooden beams. They bind his feet and then his wrists. The binding is very tight. It's so tight that his hands are already starting to lose their color.

One of the sentries steps forward and removes his helmet. His head is bald and he sports no facial hair. He stretches out his arms as if he's about to embrace the air in front of him in a bear hug and grins. "Dearly beloved, we are gathered here today…" He pauses, still grinning, and slowly examines the crowd. His grin fades and his arms slowly fall to his side. "All of you know damn well why we're here. The rules aren't hard to follow. If you keep them, you live. If you break them, you pay the price. It's not complicated. You…" He points to a man in the crowd. "Do you think this is a fair deal?"

"Yessir, it's a very fair deal," the man says with a quivering voice.

"And how about you," the sentry says, pointing to a woman in the crowd.

"It's fair. The rules are easy to follow."

The sentry looks over the crowd and his gaze stops. "You," he says and points into the crowd. Several people step aside. "That's right, you." He's pointing at a little boy. He couldn't be much older than five, maybe six at the most. His hair looks like a dirty mop. His clothes are torn and dirty. His nose is dripping snot. "Come here; it's all right." The little boy moves closer to the sentry.

The sentry kneels, lowering his height to that of the boy's. "What's your name, young man?"

"Ben."

"Ben, I want to ask you something. Do your parents have rules that you have to follow?"

The boy shakes his head in the affirmative.

"Do you follow your parent's rules?"

The boy looks behind him as though he's looking for someone, maybe one of his parents.

"Ben?" the sentry says.

"Mommy says I should always follow the rules," the boy says. He puts both hands in his pockets and looks down to the ground.

The sentry looks up at the crowd and then back to the boy. "Mommy says you should follow the rules. It sounds like you have a very smart mommy." The boy takes a hand out of his pocket and wipes snot from his nose. "Tell me, Ben. What happens when you don't follow the rules?"

The boy doesn't respond. He just looks up and stares at the sentry.

"What happens, Ben?"

"I get punished."

The sentry stands up. He seems pleased with the boy's answer. "Thank you, Ben." The boy runs back to his original spot in the crowd. The sentry looks out into the crowd. "Ben says he gets punished when he breaks the rules. You see, it's so simple even a young boy can understand it, and that brings us again to why we're here today." The sentry looks in the direction of the man strapped to the wooden cross on the ground. "This man broke the rules, and that means there must be a punishment."

The sentry turns his attention to the two men assisting in the crucifixion. "Proceed with the punishment." He then turns back to the crowd. "Let this be a lesson to all of you!"

The two men try to lift the man off the ground, but the weight of the wooden cross with the condemned man is too much for them. Several men from the crowd step forward to assist. The men lift the cross and drag it a short distance to a hole in the ground dug earlier. They insert the cross into the hole, and then with a great effort they lift it upright. It falls into the hole and lands with a thud. The condemned man moans loudly as the tendons and ligaments in his arms are pulled and stretched. He struggles to breathe.

There's a commotion in the crowd. Several people step aside and a small woman runs up to the sentry and grabs his arm.

"No! Oh, please!" she says. "Not my husband, please! I won't make it without him, I'm begging you." Tears are pouring down her anguished face.

"Get this woman off of me," the sentry says as he pushes her away.

"He's a good man! Please!" The woman says as she reaches to grab the sentry's arm again.

The sentry backhands her hard across her face and she falls to the ground. A woman from the crowd steps forward to help her up. "There's nothing you can do," I hear her say.

She helps the crying woman stand up. Another man from the crowd comes over and takes her other arm. Just as he does, the crying woman goes limp in their arms, as if her body just gave out. They drag her away from the sentry to the back of the crowd as she continues to cry and wail. Her cries of anguish are loud and my heart breaks for her, but there's not much any of us can do. If we did, we would be risking our own lives. I am disgusted by the scene taking place before me.

"If any of you offer assistance to this man, you will receive the same punishment," the sentry says. "Now go home. Show's over."

The crowd slowly starts to disburse. I see the same two people who helped the crying woman a moment ago carry her limp body away, her feet dragging the ground. She is still wailing, "no, please, why, help me," and other things. It will take her a long time to recover from this, if she ever does. These things tend to destroy entire families. I've seen it happen before. There's never a happy ending. First, someone is condemned and killed. Then, the spouse loses her will to live and dies, often by her own hand. Such an experience is enough to drive anyone mad. Any children left eventually die of starvation and general neglect. All of it is ugly.

I hear a loud sound, the report of a gunshot, off in the distance. I look in the direction of the sound but see nothing. Several people in the crowd who are still looking at the condemned man gasp in horror. I turn and look at him to see what has caught their attention. I see a hole in the center of his chest and a large amount of blood pouring from it. His body looks lifeless.

"Mercy for the condemned!" I hear someone yell in the distance. I look again in the direction of the voice but again see no one.

"Disburse, all of you!" The lead sentry says as he puts his helmet back on. The other sentry starts running in the direction of the gunshot with his rifle ready for action. The lead sentry follows closely behind.

I take one last look at the now dead man hanging on the cross. His death was meaningless, senseless. I'm not sure how much more of this the outlanders can take. I'm not sure how much more I can take. I start walking home again. The pain meds Dr. Bradshaw gave me are still working. I'm still free of pain, but I'm no longer feeling euphoric.

CHAPTER 7

I WALK THROUGH THE FRONT door of my home, glad to finally be here. It's been a very challenging day to say the least. Juno runs up and greets me, her tail wagging furiously. She puts her two front paws up on one of my legs and barks, as if to say she's happy to see me. I bend down and scratch her head with my free hand.

"Hey girl," I say. "I've missed you, too."

Mom comes over and takes the rat I'm carrying. "I see you've brought something for us. I'll start preparing it right away. Sarah picked some fiddleheads earlier that will go nicely with this. We'll have a very nice meal this evening."

A rat isn't exactly something worth getting excited over, but Mom would never complain. I know she loves me too much to ever say anything. And besides, she knows how tough things are now. Having something to eat always beats having nothing.

Sarah looks up to me from a hunched position on the floor. She's washing clothes in a tub. With our limited allotment of electricity, we haven't used a washing machine in ages.

"Tough day at the office?" she asks with a hint of a smile.

"Positively brutal. I secured three new contracts for the company and my boss had the nerve to chew me out for missing the fourth. And that's on top of having to deal with my secretary hitting on me all day long. What's a man to do? They just don't value me. I'm asking for a raise tomorrow."

Sarah tries to hold back laughter but can't. It comes out like the breaking of a levee that's been holding back more than it can stand. "You goof," she says.

I walk over to the wood stove and stoke the fire. It's going to be a cold night and we're going to need a good fire to see us through. Flames burst from the burning embers. I throw a fresh piece of wood on the fire and close the stove door. Its warmth feels good to my tired and beaten body. I sit on the floor in front of it and take it in.

Sarah continues scrubbing the laundry she's been washing. She's a hard worker. She'll make a great wife for some lucky young man some day, if that day ever comes. It's looking increasingly unlikely and I can't help but feel for her. How would she ever survive if anything ever happened to me? I don't think she would. I think that's my greatest fear...that something would happen to me and then Sarah and Mom wouldn't be able to take care of themselves. I don't worry for myself necessarily, but for them.

"Dinner is served," Mom says. I snap out of my ruminations and see Mom placing a tray of food on our small table. *My mind has been wandering longer than I realized,* I think. I get up off the floor and make my way over to the table. Sarah is right behind me. We all sit down together, but that's where the formalities end.

We attack our food like a pack of hungry wolves that hasn't eaten in days, which isn't too far from the truth. And it even tastes good, too. I don't know what kind of seasoning Mom has used on the meat, but it's quite good. For several minutes, we eat in near silence with the sounds of our forks hitting our plates being the only sounds heard.

After a few minutes of gorging, my belly starts to feel satisfied and I am acutely aware of the awkward silence.

"They punished another man today," I say in an attempt to spark a little conversation. "I'm not sure why."

Mom drops her fork on her plate, making a loud sound and causing Sarah to jump in her seat. "Must we talk about such things while we're eating?" she says.

"What do you want to talk about then? What else is there?"

"I don't know…happy things."

"Like what?"

Mom pauses with a strained look on her face, as if she is struggling to come up with something. And then I see it…a single tear falls from one of her eyes. She sighs hard, shakes her head, and more tears are now flowing. "I can't even think of anything happy. I don't know what happiness even is anymore."

Sarah goes over and puts her arms around her mother. "We're all together. That's something to be happy about, isn't it?"

"It is, baby," Mom says. "It is. I don't know what I would do without either of you. I want you both to promise me right now that you'll always be careful and that you won't do anything to ever break our family apart. Sarah?"

Sarah squeezes her mom harder. "I promise. I would never do anything like that."

"Adam?"

"Of course I promise. You guys are all I've got, too. I wouldn't do anything to ever jeopardize that."

Mom looks relieved and wipes the tears from her face. She even smiles a little. "A happy thought? Okay, how about this…Florida!" Her smile grows even wider.

"Oh, now that *is* a happy thought," I say. "Just think, no more cold winters. We could have a little place near a beach somewhere."

"And eat seafood!" Sarah says.

"Absolutely," I say. "All you can eat. I'm sure the oceans still have plenty of fish in them. And lobsters and crabs, too. Don't forget about those yummy dishes."

"Mmmmm," Sarah says while rubbing her belly. "I just ate and you're making me hungry all over again."

"Maybe we could do it," I say. "Figure out a way to make the trip down there."

"Oh, Adam," Mom says. "I don't know how we could possibly—"

"I'm serious. It might be possible. Look, I'm not saying it would be easy but we could—"

"We don't know what dangers lie between here and there. We don't even know if things would be better than they are here once we got there."

"All of that may be true, but we would never know unless we try. What if they *are* better?"

Mom gets up and walks over to me. She puts her arm around me and squeezes my body close to hers. "It's a nice thought, baby." She takes the remaining scraps of meat off our plates—what little is left, that is—and puts them in Juno's bowl. Juno attacks her meager meal.

I walk over, lean down, and scratch Juno's ears while she's chewing. She looks so emaciated and sickly. "We've got to put some meat on you, old girl. You can't be much of a guard dog like this. Can't see you scarin' off anyone in your condition. I'll see if I can get a little something extra for you next time, okay?" Juno turns, puts her front paws on my knee and licks my face. I almost wish she hadn't. Her breath is awful.

"You up for a game of Rummy?" Sarah asks, holding up a deck of cards. "You still owe me from last time."

"No can do, Sis. I ran into Dr. Bradshaw earlier and he invited me to some kind of meeting this evening. You remember Dr. Bradshaw, don't you?"

"How can I ever forget the size of that needle he injected me with that time I—"

"What's this meeting about, Adam?" Mom asks.

"I'm not entirely sure."

It's not exactly a lie since I don't know what Dr. Bradshaw has in mind. I'm afraid to tell her about what I think it's about though, not after the conversation we just had. She would worry too much. And besides, I'm not interested in joining any type of rebellion anyway if that's what he's suggesting.

"I'm mainly just going to be polite," I say.

"Maybe he's selling Amway," Sarah says.

I laugh. If it wasn't for Sarah's bubbly personality and good sense of humor, I'm not sure if I'd ever smile.

"Hard to say," I say, "but I promised him I'd be there." I get up and head for the front door.

"Maybe Elise will be there, too," Sarah says in a teasing tone of voice.

"I don't even know her, Sis. Although I'm sure she's a nice person."

"Yeah, I saw you look at—"

"That's enough, Sarah Beth!" Mom says.

"I won't be gone long," I say as I head out the door.

CHAPTER 8

MY WALK TO DR. Bradshaw's meeting is uneventful. The roads are mostly empty. I pass by the usual scenery on my way...people begging on the side of the road, abandoned buildings and cars, an empty train sitting on its tracks, a city frozen in time. As I walk past the ruins, I wonder what this place will look like a thousand years from now. Will people ever live normal lives in the city of Detroit again? Will people ever willingly move here again and raise their families in these neighborhoods? Will children ever play and laugh in the city's playgrounds again? I have no way of knowing such things, but it's hard for me to be optimistic. In time, maybe. But it's not for me to say. My crystal ball is broken.

With the eruption of Yellowstone the world purged itself of much of its population. Now an evil regime has risen in this once great city to torment the lives of those who weren't blessed to reside behind the protection of a wall, its placement seemingly arbitrary. There doesn't seem to be any sense to any of this. The people the wall protects and the people it keeps out seems so arbitrary.

For a brief moment, I have postcode envy as I wonder what kind of lives those inside the wall lead. I have no way of knowing if they have things better or worse than I do. I have never seen nor have I heard of anyone ever leaving the confines of the walls, save for the sentries. Are they prisoners or are they perfectly content in their knowledge that they are protected from the uncivilized conditions the unwashed outlanders live in? Perhaps it's a little of both.

I walk past the old Brock Comprehensive Elementary School. This is the place where I learned to read and write and to work basic math problems. It's also the place where I beat up Johnny McIntire on the playground, and where Amy Arnold gave me my first kiss behind the bleachers during play rehearsal. I was sorry for what I did to Johnny and apologized to him. We ended up becoming great friends. But I can't say I was sorry at all for what I did with Amy. She was a sweet girl. Pretty, too. I haven't heard from either of them in years and I'm not even sure if they are still alive.

The elementary school looks abandoned, like most buildings in the area. Many of its windows are shattered, no doubt from looters looking for anything they could use, eat, or maybe for a place to sleep. Its playground—the playground I formed so many memories on—is completely deserted. Its swings sit empty and still. Its monkey bars are rusting. Its grass is an unkempt, overgrown mess. The sounds of laughing, squealing children are a distant memory. For a moment, I allow myself to return to my youth and imagine myself swinging hard and high on those swings, the warm sun beating down on my face, not a care in the world. It feels so good.

I arrive at the Motor City Community Center at the appointed time and go to the back entrance as directed. I knock on the door and wait. I hear nothing. A minute passes, then two. I knock again. Silence greets me a second time. I look around to see if anyone sees me, but the back lot is empty.

There must be some mistake, I think. *Perhaps Dr. Bradshaw got his days mixed up. He did seem to be quite busy earlier.* I turn and start to walk away when I hear what sounds like footsteps on the other side of the door, and then a very small door at eye level opens. I see a pair of eyes staring at me. They look me up and then down and then the little door quickly closes. I hear the sound of a latch turning and then the door slowly opens.

A short, bald man I don't recognize is on the other side of the now open door. "You're Adam, right?" he says.

I nod my head indicating I am.

"Please, come in. We've been waiting for you."

Waiting for me? What on earth for? I wonder. *And just how did this guy know who I am?* I walk inside and he quickly closes the door behind me and then secures the lock.

"If you'll come with me," he says and then turns and starts walking down a dark, unlit hallway. I follow him. The hallway is long and it's getting so dark that I'm starting to have trouble seeing where I'm going. Just as the thought of turning around and going back to a source of light crosses my mind, we come to a closed door. I have no idea how the man could see it in such darkness, but somehow he knew to stop at just the right time. He knocks on the door in a pattern I'm certain is some kind of code. The door opens and we walk in.

The windowless room is dimly lit by many oil lamps disbursed throughout. A crowd of people is sitting, facing the opposite end of the room. I estimate their number to be somewhere between ninety and a hundred. It's a large crowd. As I walk in, they all turn around and look at me, almost on cue. I hear them whispering to each other, but I can't make out what they are saying. Most of them I don't recognize, but I do see a few familiar faces.

"What is this all about?" I whisper to the man who brought me in here.

"It's just about to begin. Take a seat, Adam."

I find an empty seat near the back of the crowd and sit down. My eyes have now adjusted to the dim lighting and I see everything much more clearly now. The room is nondescript. It is a simple room with block walls and tile flooring. There is a podium at the front of the room. The light from the many oil lanterns placed around the room casts shadows on the walls, shadows that occasionally dance from the flickering flames. I suspect the room was previously a conference room of some sort, a purpose it continues to serve today. My curiosity is now burning and I can't help but suspect I'm being let in on something very interesting.

A door on the far end of the room opens and Dr. Bradshaw enters. He leaves the door open and walks to the podium. I scan the room for Elise but don't see her.

"We've had another serious incident today, an infringement on our rights as human beings," Dr. Bradshaw says with a raised voice. There is no microphone to amplify his voice.

"He didn't deserve that!" I hear a voice from the audience say. "Nobody deserves what they did to that poor man!"

"I can't argue with you," Dr. Bradshaw says. "But it begs the question…how much more are we going to take before we start fighting back?" He looks over the crowd as he waits for a reply, but his question goes unanswered. "How much more?"

More silence.

"How many more have to die at the hands of those tyrants before we do something about it?"

"And just what army are we going to fight them with?" a man from the audience asks. "My tank is in the shop for repairs."

A wave of subtle, nervous laughter covers the room.

"We'll build an army," Dr. Bradshaw says. "We'll build an army of our bravest, brightest, and strongest."

"And just how do you propose we fight against those sentries in their ghost suits?" a woman in the audience asks. "They appear out of nowhere and terrorize us. What chance do we have against such equipment?"

"We'll just have to acquire a few of those suits for ourselves then, won't we?" The look on Dr. Bradshaw's face is serious, even though what he is suggesting sounds impossible, even laughable.

"You make it sound so easy, like we just order them from a catalog or something," another man says.

"I never said it would be easy, but it's certainly not impossible."

Several people in the audience are now whispering to each other. There is palpable tension and I sense uncertainty.

"Even if we had one of those suits for every person in this room, how do we fight them?" another woman asks. "Those suits are bulletproof and few of us have any bullets anyway."

"Only the torso is bulletproof," I say. "The designers counted on people aiming for center mass. The arms, head, and legs are vulnerable. You can hurt them, even kill them, but you've got to be either a great shot, or you have to get up close and personal to make it happen."

All heads in the room turn around and stare at me. I don't know where the words I just spoke came from. They just came out of me involuntarily, almost as if it was someone else speaking. I am embarrassed by the sudden attention and can feel my face flush. There is a long pause as everyone checks me out. It feels like an eternity, but eventually they return their gaze to the front of the room.

"Thank you, Adam," Dr. Bradshaw says. "You're absolutely right. They aren't immortal, and they certainly aren't gods. They're just people, like all of us, in protective suits, suits that we know to be vulnerable in certain areas. And they can definitely be killed."

There is a long pause and for a moment neither Dr. Bradshaw nor anyone in the room says anything. It's not hard to imagine what they must be thinking, because I'm thinking the same thing. Being free from the tyranny we now live under is a dream I'm sure we all share. I can almost see the spark of hope in their eyes. Still, it won't be an easy job, and it's apparent that some who fight against our oppressors may not live through the ordeal to realize such freedom for themselves. But their families might. My family might. It's a lot to take in and there are still many unanswered questions.

"But you still haven't explained how we fight them," a man sitting near me says. "Do you propose we shoot them with arrows? Or beat them with sticks? Maybe we should just throw stones at them. It worked for David against Goliath. Perhaps it'll work for us, too." His tone is mocking and several people respond with laughter.

Dr. Bradshaw doesn't smile. His countenance remains serious. "Yes, we will be taking on our Goliath. I won't lie to you about how difficult, or dangerous any of this will be. But I am confident that it is something that *can* be done. And to answer your question…we use guerrilla tactics. We know enough about their patrols to know with a high degree of certainty when they will be in certain areas. And they always travel in pairs, never more. We hide in the shadows and wait for them, unseen. And when they make their presence known, we sneak up behind them, slit their throats, and then quickly drag them off. Then we take their suits and use them for our purposes. We create our own army of sentry soldiers. An army we then use to overthrow this King Darius, whoever he is, and win our freedom. We do it slowly at first, eliminating only a couple of sentries every few days. If we do it slowly like this, those inside that damned wall will probably assume the sentries abandoned their posts and left the city."

"That's all well and good," the man sitting near me says, "but how do we—"

"How do we hide? We do it just like this." Dr. Bradshaw turns toward the still open door he emerged from earlier. "Elise?"

I hear faint footsteps walking from the door into the room, but there doesn't appear to be anyone there to make them. I see what I think is a faint distortion, a blur in the flickering light of the oil lanterns. It's a blur that looks very much like a...

"Sentry!" someone yells.

A loud commotion breaks forth from the crowd. Several people abruptly stand up in anticipation of making a quick escape.

"Now, now," Dr. Bradshaw says with both hands raised. "Everyone please remain calm. There is no cause for alarm. That's enough, Elise. I think we've made our point."

In the front of the room, right beside of Dr. Bradshaw, a sentry appears.

"What kind of setup is this, Bradshaw?" a visibly upset man asks.

"There's no setup, I can assure you."

The sentry reaches up to its helmet and disconnects the cable attaching the helmet to the suit. With both hands, the sentry slowly lifts the helmet off its head and locks of long, strawberry blonde hair fall out. And then I see Elise's unmistakable face where the sentry helmet once was. I am astonished and on the edge of my seat. And yes, she looks incredibly beautiful as always, even in the dim light.

Everyone in the room is also astonished, but for reasons that are different from mine. I hear someone ask Dr. Bradshaw where he got the suit. Someone else asks how it works. Another person asks what it feels like to walk around invisible. I pay no attention to most of it, except for where the suit came from. I concentrate mostly on Elise.

Dr. Bradshaw explains that he discovered the suit in an old National Guard building in a large box underneath some other boxes while he was foraging for medical supplies. Like all things involving the government, it was probably tagged, put away for storage, and then forgotten. He says some other things, but my attention is diverted by the beauty in front of me.

"What do you think, Adam?" I hear Dr. Bradshaw ask. I quickly return my attention to him, although I have no idea what he was just discussing.

"What do I think?" I ask.

"About the plan…a war of attrition. They can't have unlimited resources behind those walls, and they can only have a certain number of sentry suits. If we can get our hands on even just a few of those suits, we can fight them. And we can win. We *will* win. What do you think, Adam?"

I am unsure about any of this. On the one hand, Dr. Bradshaw's plan does sound viable. But on the other hand, I'm not sure if I want to get involved. I've never been a troublemaker, and I'm not sure I want to become one now. I glance over at Elise and she is giving me a look of great expectation, as though she wants me to go along with it. I swallow hard.

"I think it has a strong chance of working. If no more than two sentries go missing at a time, they'll have to conclude that they simply abandoned their posts and left the city for freedom. But we'll have to do a damn good job of hiding the evidence. My only concern is how many sentries can we take down before they suspect something other than abandonment?"

"Four. Maybe six at the most," Dr. Bradshaw says. "It won't take them long to catch on. But with those suits and the one we already have, it may be enough to turn things in our favor. As for hiding the evidence, we'll bury the bodies in the middle of the night. We can't drag them far. It'll use up too much time and energy. And we can't risk drawing any attention to ourselves, either."

Dr. Bradshaw pauses and surveys the room. "Very well then. Elise and I will begin making preparations for our first attack. Naturally, it will have to be a solo venture since we currently only have one suit. If anyone wants to volunteer for the job, say so now." He pauses again but the room is silent. "I want each of you to give it some thought. It is a position of great honor. When the history books are written on what we are about to do, your name could be the one that is recorded." More silence. "Do give it some thought. We have a little more time before we begin our operations. If no one has anything else to add, this meeting is adjourned."

Everyone in the room stands up and the low rumble of many people talking at once fills the room. No doubt, they are talking about the incredible spectacle they just witnessed as well as Dr. Bradshaw's incredible plan, and whether it has a chance of success, or whether being a participant in this scheme will end up being the biggest mistake of their lives. At this point, I think the odds of success could be decided with the toss of a coin. Maybe yes...maybe no. I'm not sure I like those odds.

Most in the room head for the door. Some collect their oil lanterns first before leaving. The flickering lights suddenly dance wildly as the lanterns are moved. I see Elise leave the room through the door she came in earlier. No use sticking around any longer. It's getting late and I'd like to avoid traveling in the dark if possible. I wouldn't exactly call it safe. I follow the crowd toward the door. As I wait my turn to walk down the dark hallway, I feel a hand land on my shoulder. I turn to see who it is.

"Adam, I know we can count on you in this, can't we?" Dr. Bradshaw asks.

I hesitate to give a reply, and by the look on Dr. Bradshaw's face, I can tell that he senses my indecision. "Why did you invite me here today?" I ask. "I mean, why me when there are so many other capable men to choose from? I'm sure there are many who have more meat on their bones than I do."

"Maybe so, but there's so much more to beating these guys than physical strength. There's strength of character and a strong spirit. I see those things in you, just as I saw them in your father."

"You knew my father?" I ask. I am surprised by this revelation and want to know more. It's been so long since Dad passed away, and I sometimes struggle to see his face in my memories. Sometimes I feel like I barely knew him.

"I did. He was a good man and a good friend. He was a man I always trusted. You look a lot like him, you know."

"That's what Mom says."

"And I see a lot of the same spirit he had in you. Adam, what is it you want in life?"

I don't hesitate to give an answer. It's a question I've been dwelling on for a very long time. "To live a life of peace, for Mom and Sarah to have a future, and maybe even to get married and have a family of my own someday."

"Those are worthy ambitions. But do you think you can achieve any of that the way things are now? Can you live a life of peace when you live in a state of constant fear of being beaten, or even killed for the slightest infraction?"

"No," I say flatly.

"Adam, in order to make an omelet you have to scramble some eggs. I'm not going to lie to you. What we're getting ready to do won't be easy, and some of us may not live through it. But the ends justify the means. It's time, Adam. Things have been getting much worse lately. If any of us is to have any future, we'll have to fight for it."

I nod my head in agreement. I feel like no words are necessary. He's right, of course. Things *are* getting worse. I still don't know what the answer to all of this is, but I do agree that *something* must be done if any of us is to have a future.

Dr. Bradshaw pats me on the back. "Go home. Sleep on it. No decisions need to be made this evening."

I nod again and then walk toward the dark hallway I first came through to get to this secret place. I have a strong feeling I'll be seeing it again.

CHAPTER 9

IT'S GOOD TO BE HOME. It's been a long, hard day. I walk through the front door and find Sarah and Mom reading together by the wood stove in the light of an oil lantern. There may not be any more formal schools but that hasn't stopped Mom from tutoring Sarah in various subjects...mostly the basics like reading, writing, math, and history. I have no idea what they are working on this evening.

"Power out again?" I ask.

"Yep, out again," Sarah says. "Nothing to get excited about. Nothing new, anyway."

"Indeed," I say. "Nothing new."

I walk past them to my tiny, dark bedroom, lie down, and stare at the ceiling. I let my mind go blank. It feels good to take a moment and not think about anything, to give myself a moment of freedom from this crazy world I inhabit. I don't know how long I lie here, and I can feel myself starting to drift off, but the sound of soft footsteps brings me back. I look to see who it is. Mom places a lantern on my nightstand and then sits down on the edge of my bed. She puts her hand on my arm.

"They want to fight back, don't they?" she asks in a soft voice.

"How did you know?"

"Because it's time. People can only take so much abuse before their spirits break. I reached that point a long time ago. Maybe others are stronger than I am and are able to hold out much longer, but everyone has a limit." She looks weak and I can see great pain in her eyes. "Daily death sentences, beatings, constant threats to turn our water and electricity off, and those invisible sentries…you never know where they are going to turn up so you can never let your guard down. You can never relax. And besides, I can see it in your face. I want you and your sister to have a future, Adam. My soul is tired and I'm not going to live forever. When—"

"Don't talk like that," I say. "You're going to live forever if I have anything to do with it."

"Everyone has a date with death," she says. "Dying is very much a part of living. I don't fear death, but when my time comes I do want to go with the knowledge that you and your sister have a much better future than what we have now."

"What we have now is fine," I say. "You know I don't care about material possessions."

"That's not what I'm talking about. I'm not talking about living in a fancy home, or wearing fancy clothes, or any of that. I'm talking about living a life that is free. Don't you want to be able to go about your daily activities without living in constant fear of being attacked by one of those goons in their suits?"

"Of course that's what I want." And it really is. I want very much to be able to get married someday and to have a family of my own. And I want the same for Sarah. But I also know these things can't possibly happen in the environment we currently live in. It weighs heavily on my heart.

"How are they going to do it? Fight them, I mean?" Mom asks.

"They got their hands on one of those suits," I say in a lowered voice. I doubt anyone can hear our conversation but I lower my voice anyway. "Bradshaw wants us to use it to take out more sentries to get their suits. I'm not sure exactly what he's got in mind after that. Some kind of big attack, I assume."

"That sounds like the best plan I've heard so far. It sounds risky, but doable. Especially—"

"Dr. Bradshaw mentioned something tonight that I didn't know," I say. "He said he and Dad used to be good friends. Why hasn't anyone ever mentioned that before?"

Mom turns her gaze from me to the wall beside me as if she's in deep thought. She takes in a deep breath and then slowly exhales. "Yes, they were good friends...best friends, you could even say. They grew up together, but things were a little strained between them in the years before your father passed away."

"What happened?" I ask.

Mom takes another deep breath and holds it for a moment before slowly letting it out. "Me."

"You?"

"Me. I'm what happened."

"What do you mean? What on earth are you talking about?"

"Both your father and Dr. Bradshaw were in love with me at the same time many years ago. It caused a bit of a rift in their friendship. They didn't exactly stop being friends, but they did stop spending as much time together as they used to. Of course, that was a long time ago, and he wasn't a doctor in those days, either."

I can understand why Mom never mentioned it before. It's not exactly the type of thing that makes for great dinner conversation. And it's not something a mother would normally discuss with her children, either. But now my curiosity is burning and I want to know more. "Why did you choose Dad over Dr. Bradshaw?" I ask. "How did Dad win?"

The look on Mom's face softens and I even detect a hint of a smile, as if she's remembering better times. "Your father pursued me... relentlessly. He did everything right. He courted me like it was his job, and he did that job very well. But it wasn't just that. Your father and I were made for each other, Adam. I'm sure of it. Your father was my best friend. It was one of those things that was just meant to be."

"And what of Dr. Bradshaw?"

"Richard Bradshaw is a good, decent man. I would've done well to marry him. There's no question about that. But your father is the man I fell in love with. My heart would always melt when I would look into his brown eyes. You've got his eyes, you know."

"I don't know about that."

"Well, I do," she says and leans in and kisses my forehead. "You get some rest now. You've earned it." She gets up, retrieves the lantern, and starts walking toward the bedroom door.

"Mom?"

She turns around just as she's about to walk through the door. "Yes, dear."

"What I was talking to you about earlier... Florida. I wasn't joking. I really think we could do it. If we—"

"I know you weren't joking, but not right now...not with winter almost here. I'd turn into a Popsicle out there the first time it snows.

We both laugh.

"I'll tell you what. Talk to me about it again in the spring. Maybe it really is something we can make happen. I've always wanted to live near a beach." She smiles and then turns and walks out of the room.

I continue to stare at the ceiling and think about what life in Florida would be like. And oh, what a great thought it is. Warm weather. My bare feet walking on the hot sands of some beach. Sunsets. In my mind, I'm already there. Mind over matter. I drift off to sleep.

CHAPTER 10

I OPEN MY EYES AND LET the world around me come into focus. It's morning. I must have slept very soundly. I'm not even sure if my body moved in my sleep. Extreme fatigue will do that. As my senses continue to awaken, I am suddenly aware of the sound of heavy breathing next to me. I'm pretty sure I know what the source is, but I turn and look anyway and find myself face-to-face with Juno's snout. Her large tongue hangs lazily from her open mouth. I reach up and scratch her ears.

"Hey girl," I say. She licks the side of my face. Normally this would not be something I would want to start my day with, but for some reason this morning I don't mind. She places her head on my chest and I continue to scratch her ears. "Did you sleep well, too?"

I feel invigorated, rejuvenated, and I suspect there's much more to it than merely getting a good night's sleep. I sense a feeling I haven't felt in a long time. In fact, I've almost completely forgotten what it even feels like. It's a feeling of…hope.

I feel hopeful of actually having a future for the first time in ages. And oh, what a beautiful, warm feeling it is. Dare I dream? Yes, I dare. A family of my own. A wife and children. A home of our own. To someday laugh and play with my own grandchildren. A future for Sarah. To see my mother genuinely happy again. Real hope. And why not?

Who says I have to accept my fate as some kind of servant slave? Who says I, or any one of us, must continue to live bleak lives of uncertainty? I realize I have a clear choice: I can accept a life where I merely react to the things that happen around me and to me, or I can forge a new future based on the actions I take in the present. It really isn't a difficult decision. I know what I have to do.

"Time to get up, Juno," I say. She quickly gets up and jumps off the bed, as if she understood me. There are times when I think she really does. I practically jump out of bed myself and quickly throw myself together. I throw my clothes on, brush my teeth, and run a comb through my hair. There's no time for perfection today. I am a man on a mission.

I rush through the house and head straight for the door. Sarah and Mom are already up. I pay no attention to them as I get ready to leave.

"I was wondering when you were going to roll out of bed," Sarah says. "Do you know what time it is?"

"It's time for action," I say as I grab my hunting knife and strap it on. Sarah rolls her eyes.

"Where are you going?" Mom asks.

"I'm going to catch up with Dr. Bradshaw. There's something important I need to tell him."

"Are you..." Mom pauses. She doesn't even need to finish her question. I see anticipation in her eyes.

"Yes," I say. The look on Mom's face speaks volumes. It's a look that says she is pleased with my decision.

"You need to eat an egg before you leave. I can't let you leave this house on an empty stomach."

"You worry too much."

"Isn't that what mothers are supposed to do?"

"Maybe so, but you're a professional." I take her by the shoulders, lean in, and kiss her cheek. "I won't be gone long." I turn and walk out the door, the first steps taken toward a new future.

CHAPTER 11

THE DAY IS UNUSUALLY BRIGHT. A few rays of sunshine are piercing the veil of the thick blanket of cloud cover that normally hangs overhead. There's a strong breeze blowing and the clouds are moving. An occasional hole in the clouds allows the sun to shine through, and I can actually see the old fireball in the sky. Beautiful. Warm. It's like seeing an old friend again. *Don't be such a stranger, okay?*

I start walking on the main road to my destination. I don't travel far until I pass by two young boys playing by the side of the road on an old abandoned Chevy Impala. The boys are filthy and don't look like they've bathed in weeks, maybe months. The Impala looks like it's seen better days. It's old…a 73 model, I think. I never did learn my GM cars that well. It's so big, it almost looks like you could stick a mast in its hull and sail it down the river…almost. But not this old bucket of rust and holes. Those kids are only one scrape or cut away from catching tetanus and dying because of that old thing.

One of the kids watches me as I pass by. I try not to pay them any mind. He points at me and makes the shape of a gun with his finger and thumb. "Pow!" he says. "You're a dead man!"

I keep walking.

"Sentries gonna get you!" I hear the other boy say.

"Citizen, halt!" the other boy says. They both erupt in laughter.

Real funny, you little shits, I think. *Tetanus might be too good for the two of you.*

I keep walking and get far enough away from them that I no longer hear their taunts, but I don't get too far until something catches my attention. In the distance on the road ahead, I see two sentries appear in front of an old man. This doesn't look good. I step to the side of the road, crouch down behind an abandoned truck, and pretend to adjust my boots.

I see them talking but I'm too far away to hear what they are saying. The elderly man throws his hands up in the air. It's not hard to speculate on what I'm witnessing. The sentries are accusing him of something. It doesn't matter what. I'm sure it's nothing of significance. The accused man is denying it. I've seen this scenario play out more times than I care to count.

One of the sentries pulls out his baton and starts beating the old man. After only two hits, he falls to the ground. I don't see him moving anymore, but apparently that isn't enough for the sentry, as he beats the man's lifeless body some more. Over and over again, he delivers his blows. The old man looks frail and I'm not sure this is something he'll live through. Perhaps it's best for him that he meets his end quickly instead of the slow, excruciating method of crucifixion the sentries have been using.

My heart breaks for the old man but I know I can't intervene. To do so would be inviting unwanted attention, even my own death. I feel enraged at what I am seeing, at what has been going on for far too long. *How could I have been such a fool?* I wonder. *How could I ever have thought that I could have any sort of life the way things are?* To say that things have been bad is the understatement of the century. And now, things are going from bad to worse.

The people can't take this anymore. I can't take this anymore. I am now more certain than ever of my decision to join Dr. Bradshaw in his attempt to do something about this insanity. What have I got to lose...my life? I now realize that it's just a matter of time before my card is drawn and they accuse me of some sort of crime against King Darius. It's not a matter of *if* at this point...but *when*. It's eventual. It could happen tomorrow for all I know, or maybe next week. No, this isn't a life at all. It's little more than an existence. I will win freedom from this tyranny for my family and me, or I will die trying to obtain it.

I stand up from my crouched position and continue walking. The sentries have stopped hitting the old man. Why continue? There doesn't appear to be any life left in him to torment at this point. I'm all but certain he's dead. I cut down an alley between two buildings. What little sunshine there is today doesn't penetrate this dark, ominous place. A few small rats scurry away as I pass through this desolate area. It smells. The stench is strong, and the smell of urine, feces, and rotting dead animals burns my nostrils. I move quickly past mounds of filth. It's much easier to travel on the main road, but I'm willing to endure the alleys and back roads if it means avoiding any unnecessary entanglements.

The alley comes to an end and opens up to an old residential area. The homes here appear to be abandoned. Most of them no longer have windows, their glass panes long ago smashed by looters. Still, one can never be too sure these days. Shelter is shelter when you don't have a place to call your own. I take a moment and scrape the sole of one of my shoes against a rock. I've managed to pick up something sticky and gooey and I don't even want to know what it is. I'm not far from Dr. Bradshaw's home at this point. I'm thankful it's a short trip. The less time I spend out in the open, the better.

I cut through the backyard of one of the homes and climb a fence to get to the other side. I wade through the marsh of wet, uncut grass that used to be a lawn. I come to a back road and take it, following my internal compass as I go. I cut through another back alley and then down a narrow path along an embankment. I can now see my destination. Dr. Bradshaw's house is just ahead. I start walking toward it and then I see her...

I see Elise not far from me up the road carrying a bundle of sticks. She's been gathering wood for the evening fire. This is my opportunity to talk to her! What better way to break the ice than to tell her I'll be joining her father to fight back against our oppressors. She'll be glad to hear it; I'm sure of it. I can already imagine it in my mind. I'll tell her the good news and then watch the expression of happiness form on her face. She might even give me a big hug. She'll tell me how glad she is that I've decided to join them, and then I'll act like it's no big deal. "It's the right thing to do," I'll say calmly. Then she'll escort me to her home, chatting on the way, where we'll tell Dr. Bradshaw together.

Are these the thoughts of a delusional man? Perhaps. But a man can dream, can't he? I'll know soon enough, anyway. I'm not far from her now, just a few homes away. I should probably be a gentleman and offer to carry the bundle of sticks she's carrying, too. Yes, I'll do that. I see her crouch to pick up another stick and then...

"No!" I say to myself as a sentry suddenly appears in front of her. I continue walking toward her. I don't take cover this time. My legs seem to be operating on autopilot, as if they are completely disengaged from my brain.

I see Elise shake her head in the negative. The sentry has said something to her, accused her of something and she is denying it. She slowly takes a couple of steps back. I feel anger building inside of me. I am walking a little faster now. Elise looks in my direction. Her eyes meet my eyes. She knows I'm here. My pace quickens a little more.

The sentry moves quickly toward her and grabs her arm, causing the load of wood she is carrying to fall to the ground. I am now in a slow run. The anger inside me grows. The sentry removes his helmet and tosses it aside. He grabs Elise's other arm. She's squirming now.

The sentry pulls hard on her arms, forcing her body close to his. He is much larger than she is, and much stronger. He grabs her waist with one arm and holds her body against his. She is trying to resist but it's no use. She is overpowered. I am now running fast and hard. The rage inside me has now completely taken over. The sentry takes his free hand and pulls her dress up, exposing her.

"No!" I yell loudly and grab the sentry from behind. I wrap one arm around his neck and the other around his waist. He immediately releases Elise. She takes a few steps back, stumbles, and falls to the ground. I've surprised him. He didn't see or hear me coming, but he quickly grabs the arm I have around his waist and pulls it off him. He is very strong.

I jump on his back, putting all of my weight on him. I grab his waist again. This throws him off balance and he takes a couple of wobbly steps to regain his footing. I tighten my grip on the arm I have around his neck and can feel him struggling to breathe.

For a moment neither of us moves. The sentry grabs the arm I have around his neck and tries to pull it off, but I can tell that he is losing his strength. I feel my grip slipping. My strength is fading as well...my hunting knife!

I release my grip on his waist and reach for the hunting knife strapped to my leg. It slides out of its sheath. In an instant, I release the sentry's neck and grab his hair, pulling his head back swiftly and sharply. I run my hunting knife across his neck, nearly decapitating him.

The sentry's body goes limp and falls to the ground. A pool of blood is forming underneath his body. The sight in front of me is surreal. I just took a life. It's as though it just happened to someone else and I am a spectator watching from a distance. I feel disconnected from my own body. Blood covers my hands and my knife. I don't see Elise.

I look around to see if I see her or if anyone has seen what I just did. I'm alone. I see no one. I wipe the blade and put it back in its sheath. I have to do something with the body quickly before someone finds out. I don't know what I'm going to do with it, maybe drag it off somewhere and hide it. I reach down to grab the body.

"Don't move!" I hear from behind me in a loud voice. I slowly stand up and turn around. A sentry is pointing his rifle at me. He's close, but not close enough to hit me without being a good shot. If he captures me, I'm a dead man, no question about it. I have only one option…

I run.

CHAPTER 12

I RUN FAST AND HARD. I feel a surge of adrenaline course though my body and I run with everything in me, like a frightened gazelle running from a hungry cheetah. I hear a gunshot from behind me and see the impact of the round on a brick building in front of me. Much too close for comfort. I run even faster.

It's amazing what the human body can do when confronted with life or death situations. Some say the body can do superhuman things in such instances. I say it's just a matter of survival. Either we do or we die.

Another gunshot goes off behind me. Another round hits the ground in front of me. I glance behind me and see the sentry running every bit as hard as I am, holding his rifle out in front of him with both hands. He's closer than I thought he would be. He's fast.

I run down a side alley. If I can't outrun him, I'll have to try to lose him or hide from him. I jump over some debris and keep running. I look behind me again and don't see him, although I'm sure he saw me go this way. There's not much time to lose him.

I quickly climb on top of a dumpster and try to reach the roof of the building beside it. I could lose him if I could climb up there without being seen. I stretch my entire body and stand on my toes, but I'm not tall enough to grab hold of the edge of the roof. I jump hard and the ends of my fingers grab hold of the gutter. I don't have a good grip and I can feel my fingers slipping, slipping...

I hear another gunshot and this one is loud, the narrow alley no doubt amplifying the report. The bullet ricochets just inches in front of me off the wall in front of my face. Startled, I lose my grip and come down hard on the dumpster below. My body rolls off the angled dumpster lid and I land with a thud on the ground. There's not a second to spare. I quickly pull myself up and continue running from my pursuer.

I've lost precious ground with my attempt to climb on the roof and the sentry is now much closer. I can even hear his footsteps running behind me. My breathing is labored and my lungs are burning. My heart is beating so fast I think I can hear it. I'm running slower now. I'm tiring, and I can only hope and pray that my pursuer is tiring, too.

My legs and feet feel so heavy, like I'm trying to lift large bags of sand with each step I take. I don't even know where I'm running to, only that I'm running away. All of this shooting is loud and I fear that it's drawing a lot of unwanted attention. I don't stand a chance if I happen upon another pair of sentries.

I hear another gunshot behind me and a window shatters in front of me. I glance behind me again but my pursuer is not as close as he was. He's losing ground. His external appearance may be intimidating, but on the inside he is a human being, someone who can't run at full speed indefinitely.

I turn a corner and head down another alley. Almost immediately, I see a set of stairs leading down to the basement of some building. I run down them and turn the doorknob. It turns but the door doesn't open. I hear my pursuer's footsteps in the distance. I turn the knob again and push hard against the door with my shoulder, putting all of my weight behind it. I can feel the door give a little, like it's trying to open but it just doesn't have the proper motivation. The footsteps are getting much closer... much louder.

I take a step back and hit the door hard with my shoulder. It opens and my body falls into the room and lands on the floor. I quickly jump up and push the door closed, nearly tripping over my own feet. The room is dark and I frantically feel for a lock but can't find one. My breathing is so loud I'm afraid it can be heard through the walls, through the door in front of me, but I can't help it. My body is sucking in air hard and fast to compensate for the punishment I just put it through.

There's a small grime-covered window at ground level that I can barely see through, but I can see just well enough to make out the sentry's feet as he slowly runs by my hiding place. I stand there with my hand on the door knob and my shoulder pushing hard against the door, fully expecting the sentry to come bursting through at any moment...but nothing happens.

I continue pushing against the door. A minute passes, then two. My breathing is slowing and my heart no longer feels like it's about to burst. I release the door handle and turn around with my back against the door. I slowly slide to the ground.

The sun is quickly going down and there's almost no light penetrating the room, only a few rays that hit the ceiling. Everything else is dark. I can see my feet in front of me but not much else. The room has a strong musty smell to it. I'll have to spend the night here. I can't possibly risk trying to make my way home after what just happened. The sentries are sure to be on high alert.

Did the sentry who chased me identify me? I don't know. If he did, what will happen to Mom and Sarah? I don't know. Is Elise okay? I don't know. My life has just taken a major detour and I know that things will never again be the same. There are so many things I am unsure of, but there's one thing I know with certainty...

I am a wanted man.

The Detroitopia saga continues!

Be sure to check out the next installment,
Wanted Man, to see what happens next!